My father
always works
with his hands.

He builds
things in his
workshop.

He measures
with his ruler,
marking the wood
with a pencil. Then
he measures again,
just to be sure.

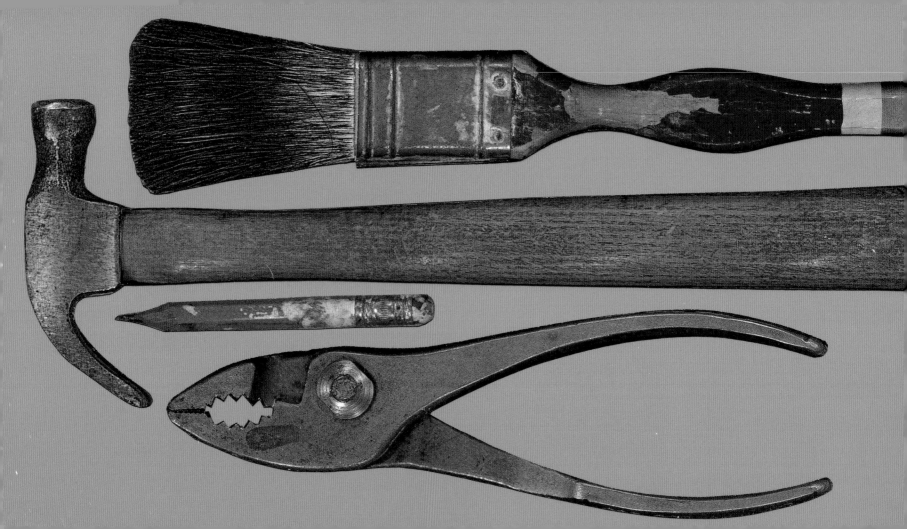

He's picky.
When I help, I try to
do things like he does.
He's showing me how
to paint, pound nails
straight, and saw wood.

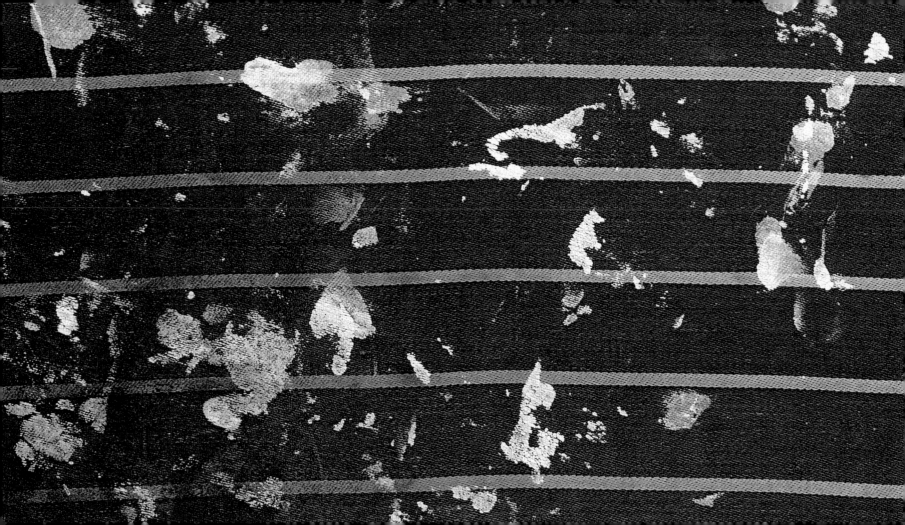

My mother
makes
things, too.

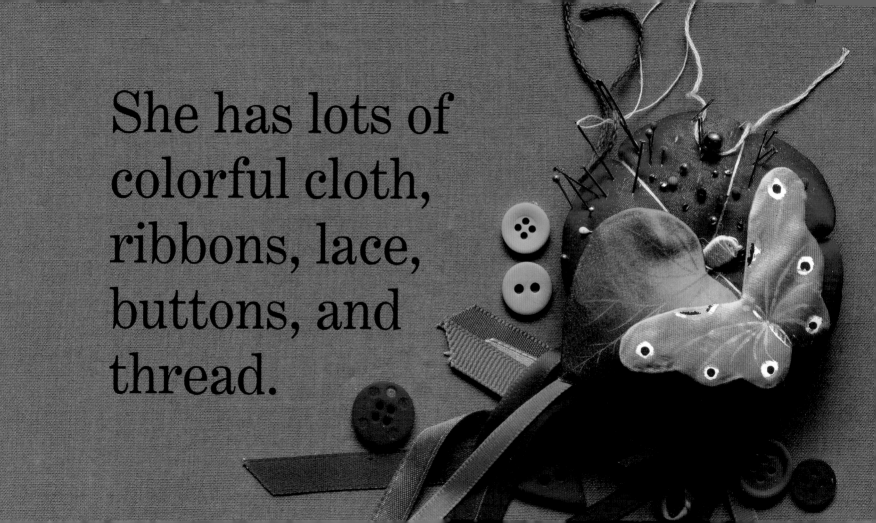

She has lots of colorful cloth, ribbons, lace, buttons, and thread.

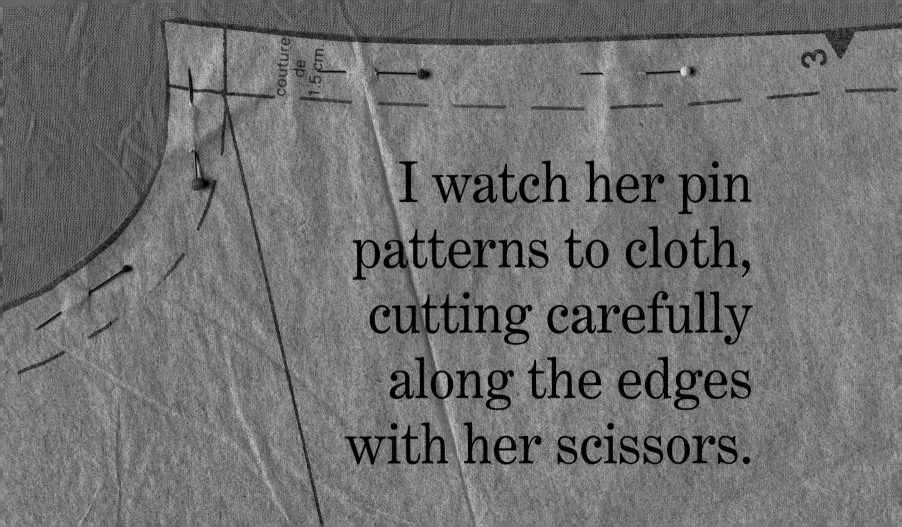

couture de 1.5 cm.

3

I watch her pin patterns to cloth, cutting carefully along the edges with her scissors.

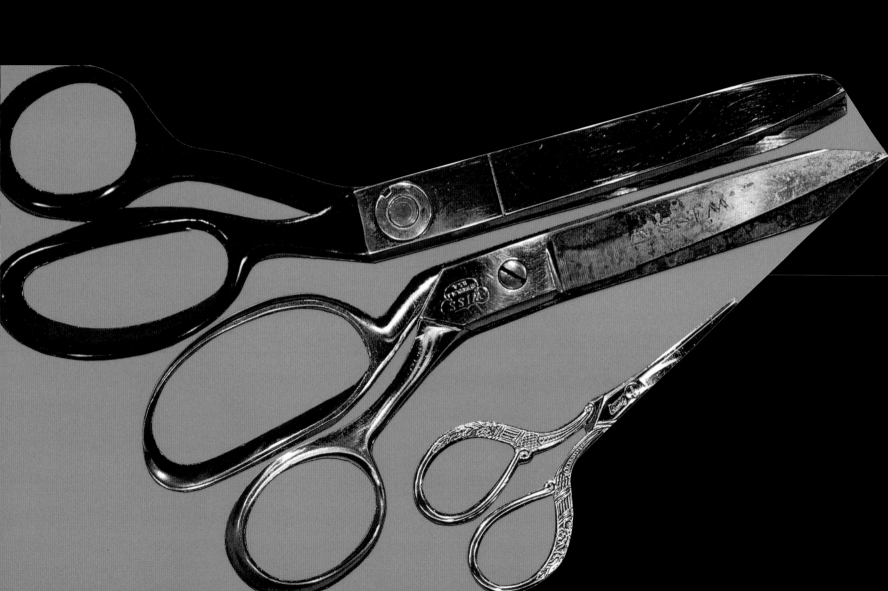

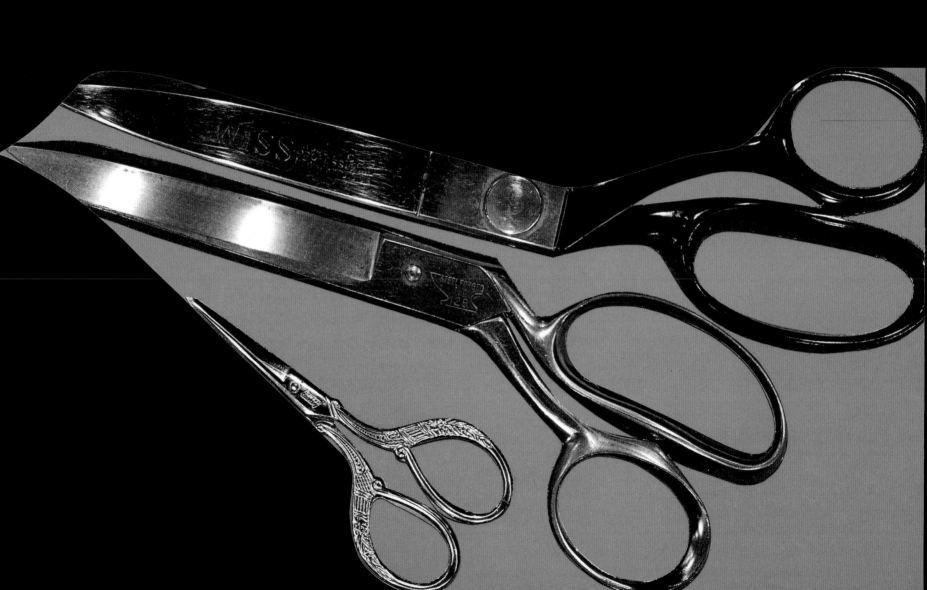

She has many scissors—
big, heavy ones and
pointy, little ones
that fit my hand.

Together we make cat toys.

Today Dad put up
a folding table
near Mom's
sewing machine.
It's for me!

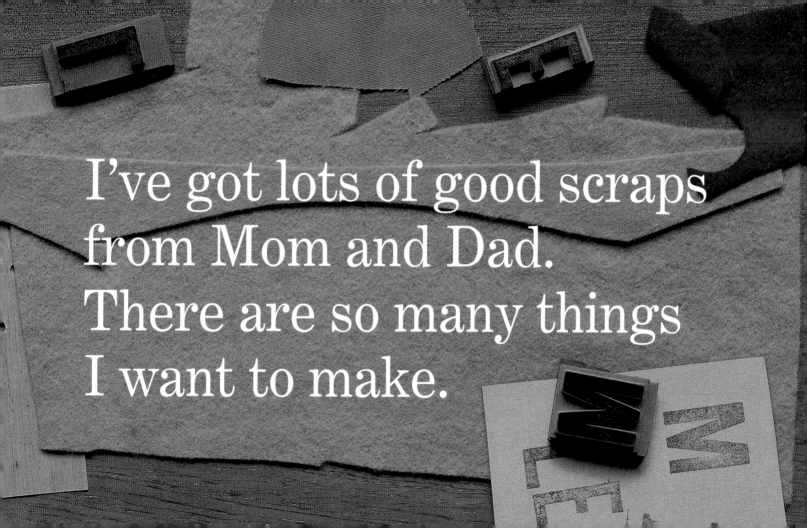

I've got lots of good scraps from Mom and Dad. There are so many things I want to make.

I just finished this pot holder for our kitchen.

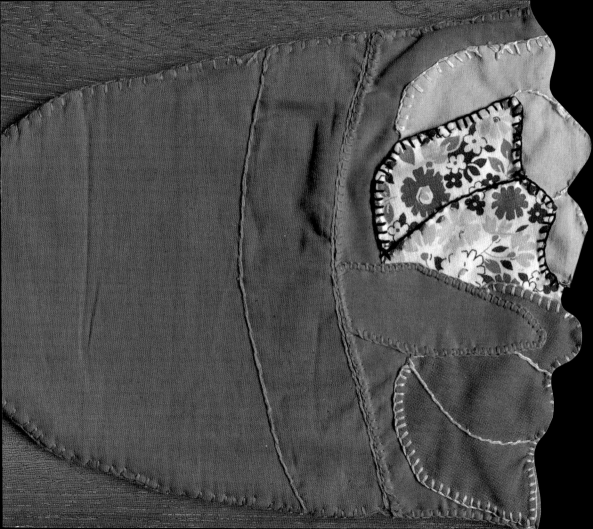

I wish
I could stay
here forever.

But I hear
Dad and Mom
calling me.
They need
extra hands
in the garden.

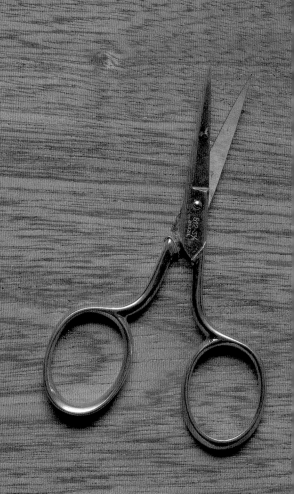

Every year
I help plant
vegetable seeds.

HEARTLAND
SEED COMPANY

Early Red
TOMATO

HEARTLAND
SEED COMPANY

Sun of Mexico
ZINNIA

Mom grows flowers.
She likes the
bright colors.
So do I.

I'm good at weeding.
Dad says I have
sharp eyes,
that I see things
other people miss.

When our
flowers bloom,
I'm going to paint
a picture of them.

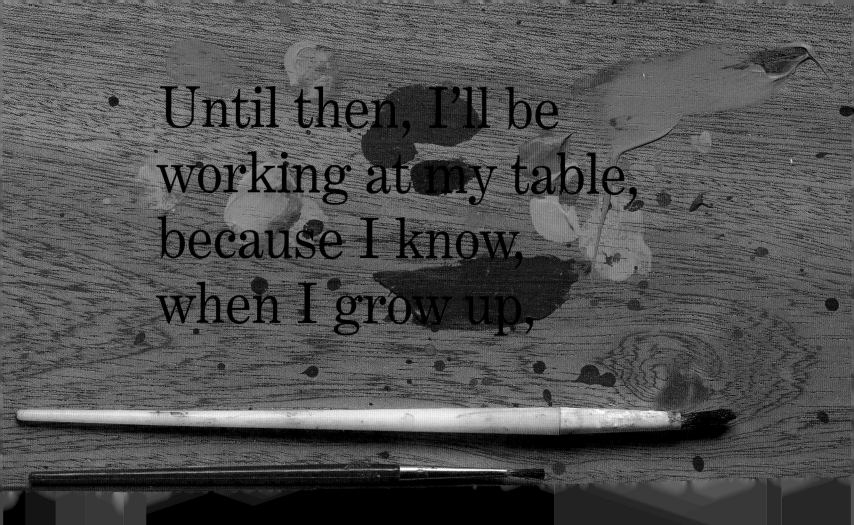

Until then, I'll be working at my table, because I know, when I grow up,

I want
to be an
artist.

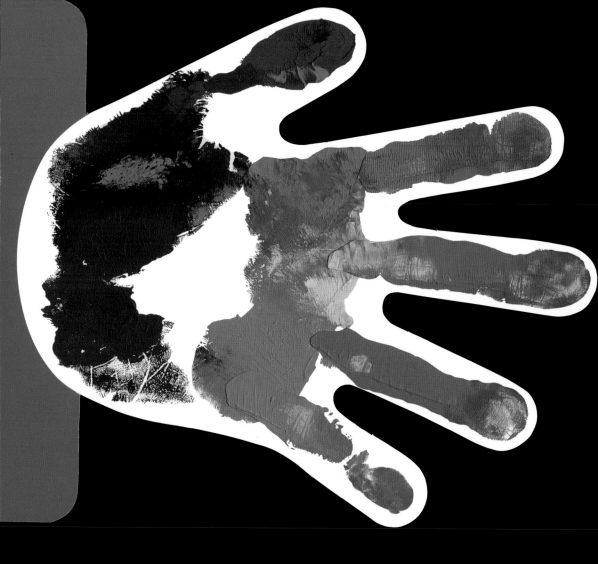

Then
I'll join
hands

with my mom

and dad.

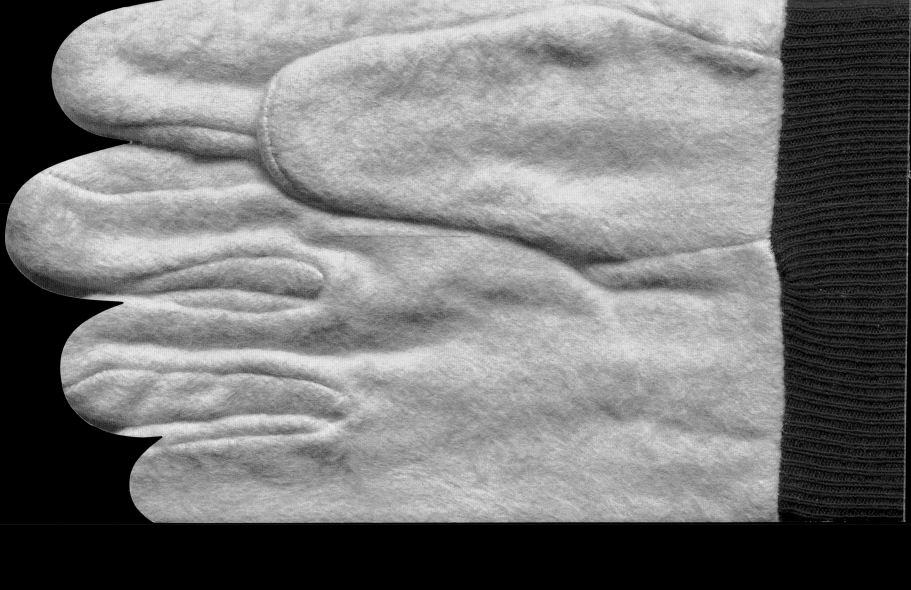

A Note from the Author

I grew up in a home where everyone was making something with their hands. As far back as I can remember, I was always putting things together—cutting, stitching, pasting, or pounding.

My mother, a good seamstress, shared her fabric scraps with me, and when I was eight, taught me how to use her sewing machine. My dad had a basement workshop from which he supplied me with lots of scrap lumber and nails. So I always had a ready supply of art materials, but not necessarily traditional ones like paper and paint.

I worked on a folding table. My mom and dad let me leave my projects spread out there as long as I wanted, so I could continue working in my free time and not worry about picking up. I'm still messy when I work. When ideas are coming, I don't clean my studio every day—I keep working. I know there will be days when I have no ideas, and then I will have plenty of time to clean up and empty my overflowing wastebasket.

My folding table was my own spot. I hope you, too, will find a spot of your own. Creativity is within all of us; we just need time—and a place—to nurture it.

www.HarcourtBooks.com

First published in 1997

Library of Congress Cataloging-in-Publication Data available upon request.
LC 2004001237

First edition
A C E G H F D B

The display and text type were set in Century Expanded.
Color separations by Bright Arts Ltd., Hong Kong
Printed and bound by Tien Wah Press, Singapore
This book was printed on totally chlorine-free Stora Enso Matte paper.
Production supervision by Sandra Grebenar and Pascha Gerlinger